AUSTRALIAN MARINE FISH

NATURE kids™

Mason Crest Publishers
www.masoncrest.com
Philadelphia

Mason Crest Publishers
370 Reed Road
Broomall, PA 19008
(866) MCP-BOOK (toll free)

First printing

ISBN 1-59084-215-4

Library of Congress Cataloging-in-Publication Data on file at the Library of Congress

First published by Steve Parish Publishing Pty Ltd
PO Box 1058, Archerfield BC
Queensland 4108, Australia
© Copyright Steve Parish Publishing Pty Ltd

Underwater Photography: Steve Parish

Front Cover: Beaked Coralfish and Cleaner Wrasse
Top, right: Eastern Smooth Boxfish. Bottom, left: Pigfish. Bottom, right: Magpie Morwong and Cleaner Wrasse (photo Steve Parish)

Printed in Jordan

Writing, editing, design, and production by Steve Parish Publishing Pty Ltd, Australia

CONTENTS

Use of Capital Letters for Animal Names in this book
An animal's official common name begins with a capital letter.
Otherwise the name begins with a lowercase letter.

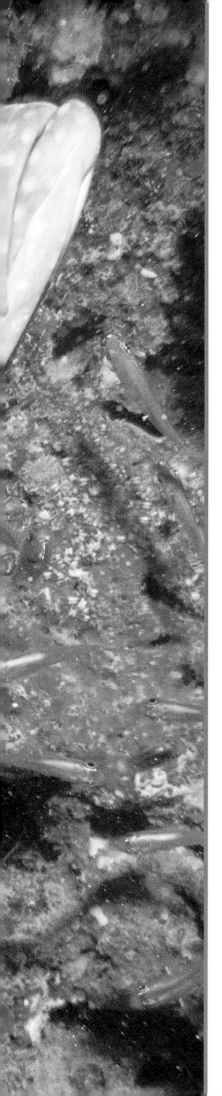

WHAT IS A FISH?

Fish are animals that live in water and breathe through gills. They use fins and tails to move.

Fish with bony skeletons have scales that overlap, like tiles on the roof of a house. Inside their bodies are swim bladders filled with gas that stop the fish from sinking.

Sharks and rays have skeletons made of cartilage. Their scales are like little teeth set in rows. They do not have swim bladders.

◀ The Coral Rockcod has a skeleton made of bone.

▲ The Whale Shark has a skeleton made of gristly cartilage. It is the world's largest fish.

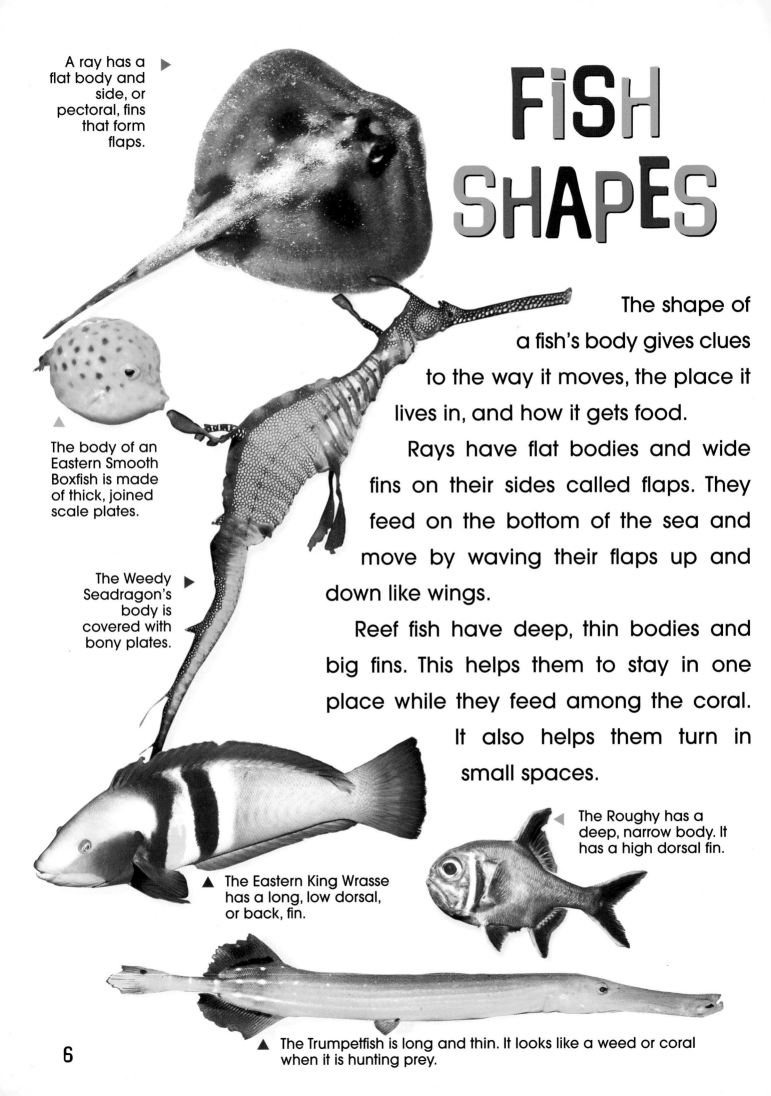

A ray has a flat body and side, or pectoral, fins that form flaps.

FISH SHAPES

The shape of a fish's body gives clues to the way it moves, the place it lives in, and how it gets food.

Rays have flat bodies and wide fins on their sides called flaps. They feed on the bottom of the sea and move by waving their flaps up and down like wings.

Reef fish have deep, thin bodies and big fins. This helps them to stay in one place while they feed among the coral. It also helps them turn in small spaces.

The body of an Eastern Smooth Boxfish is made of thick, joined scale plates.

The Weedy Seadragon's body is covered with bony plates.

The Roughy has a deep, narrow body. It has a high dorsal fin.

The Eastern King Wrasse has a long, low dorsal, or back, fin.

The Trumpetfish is long and thin. It looks like a weed or coral when it is hunting prey.

6

Truncate Coralfish

Dorsal Fin

Tail Fin

Gill Cover

Pectoral Fin

Ventral Fin

Pelvic Fin

USING FINS AND TAILS

A fish uses its fins and tail to pull and push itself through the water. Many fish can move backwards as easily as they move forwards.

Some fish have venomous spikes on the tips of their fins.

Some fins show bright colors or strange shapes when they are opened. They can be used to send signals to other fish.

◀ The Paperfish has a huge dorsal fin.

▲ The Common Lionfish can pump venom out of the tips of its dorsal fins. It uses its pectoral fins to round up prey.

▲
The Tall-fin Batfish has long fins.

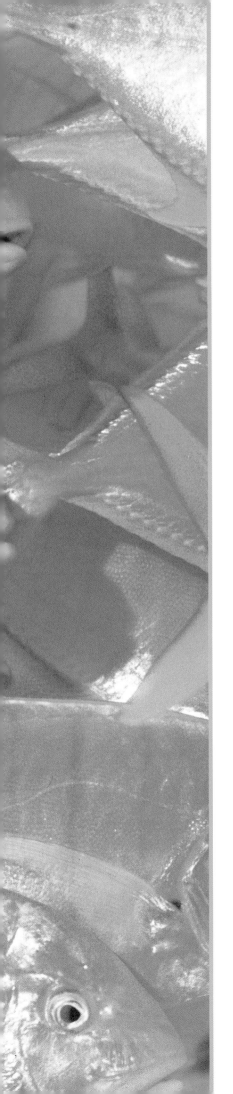

FiSH THAT SWiM FAST

Fish that live in the open ocean are fast, strong swimmers. They must swim against strong currents and tides. They also need to catch other fish to eat.

The bodies of these fast fish have no bumps, allowing them to slip smoothly through the water. They have plenty of muscle to give them power and speed.

◀ Golden Trevally often live in large groups called schools. They can swim very fast.

▲ Barracuda eat other fish. They have strong jaws and sharp teeth.

HITCHHIKERS AND HEADLIGHTS

Some small fish hitch rides on larger fish. They have ventral or dorsal fins that are joined. Together, these fins form a sucker that can cling onto the skin of another fish.

A Pineapplefish has a light on either side of its lower jaw. The light comes from tiny bacteria that grow on special patches of skin. The fish uses its lights at night to find shrimps to eat.

▲ Pineapplefish hunt shrimps at night. They spot them with the help of lights on their lower jaws.

A Senator Wrasse with a small Eastern ▶ Cleaner Clingfish hitching a ride on its tail.

FiSH COLORS

◀ A Black-Tipped Fusilier in night
▼ colors, left, and day colors,
below

Many fish are brightly colored. The colors and the patterns they form help the fish recognize each other. A young fish and an adult of the same sort may be differently colored. Also, a female and a male may have different colors.

Fish have special skin cells that allow them to change colors.

A fish may change color at night or to blend in with its surroundings to hide from enemies. When fish are ready to find mates and breed, their colors may become quite bright.

The female Pigfish, above, is differently ▲
colored from the male, below. ▼

▲ Colors help fish tell if other fish are like them or if they are of a different kind.

The Black-spot Goatfish at left have turned dark so that the Comb Wrasse can see the pests they need picked off their skins. The resting goatfish below have turned pale. The eyespots on their tails would help confuse an attacker.

▲ Black-spot Goatfish and a Comb Wrasse

Black-spot Goatfish resting: their pale colours make the eyespots on the tails stand out. ▼

▲ An Australian Fur Seal hunting fish.

SOME ENEMIES OF FISH

People catch fish in nets, on lines, and in traps. Many sorts of waterbirds feed on fish. Dolphins and seals hunt fish underwater. However, some of the greatest fish-eaters of all are other, larger fish, such as sharks.

◀ Silver Gull

◀ A group of Australian Pelicans fishing.

▲ Bottlenose Dolphins eat fish.

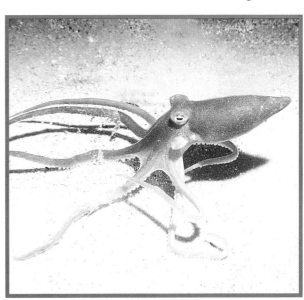

An octopus stalking fish at night. ▲

CONFUSING ATTACKERS

When a school of fish is attacked, its members group tightly together. The enemy does not know which fish to attack.

The gurnard lives on the seabed. It bluffs an attacker by spreading its fins. Its pectorals have bright rims. Its dorsal fin has a spot like a big eye. This may frighten off an enemy.

A Southern Spiny Gurnard flashing its dorsal and pectoral fins ▶ to frighten off an attacker.

▲ An enemy does not know which member of a large school of fish to attack.

▲ The Southern Spiny Gurnard lies on the sand. When an enemy comes near, it flashes bright fins to startle it.

HiDiNG FROM DANGER

Fish find hiding places that can protect them from enemies.

Anemonefish live between the stinging tentacles of sea anemones. The anemone's sting does not harm them. When danger is near, the fish darts into the middle of the tentacles.

◀ A Pink Anemonefish protected by the stinging tentacles of a sea anemone.

Damselfish hiding ▲ between the sharp spikes of staghorn coral.

▲ A tiny Blenny looking out of its hiding place in a piece of coral.

FiSH CAMOUFLAGE

▲ A Scorpionfish waiting for prey.

Camouflage coloring lets a fish blend in with its surroundings.

Fish that are hunted by other fish use camouflage to escape being eaten.

Fish that hunt other creatures to eat use camouflage to hide from their prey. Some lie very still until a victim comes within reach. Then the fish quickly opens its mouth, sucks the victim in, and gulps it down.

▲ A camouflaged Rock Cale.

▲ A Johnston's Weedfish waits to catch a small fish or other sea creature.

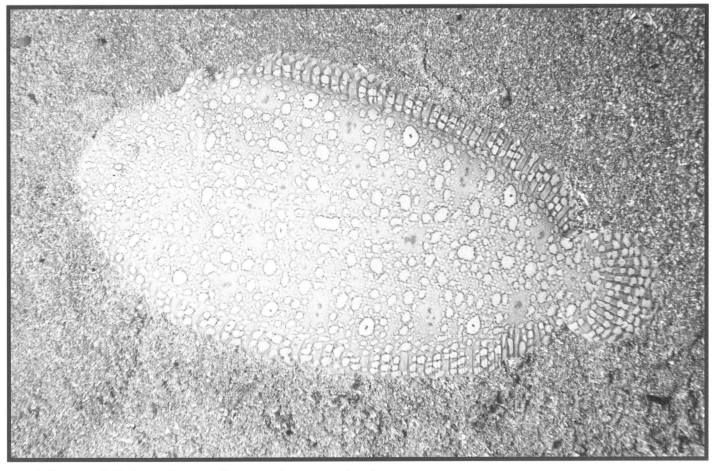

▲ A Peacock Sole resting on the sandy ocean bed.

▲ The stripes on this Blenny confuse a hunter's eye. The fish does not have a clear outline.

HOW FiSH PROTECT THEMSELVES

▲ The Mimic Filefish, left, looks like the Saddled Puffer, right, whose flesh is poisonous.

▲ The Numbfish is a small ray. It can put out an electric charge that can kill an attacker.

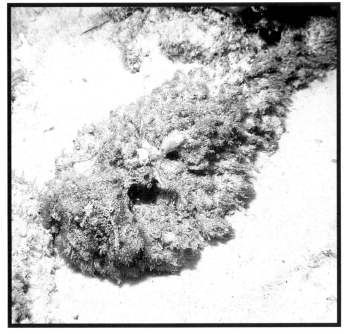

▲ A stonefish lying on the bottom waiting for prey: it has 13 venomous dorsal spines.

▲ A porcupinefish has spines on most of its body. It can puff up into a ball.

◄ The Red Rockcod has dorsal spines that can inject venom into an attacker.

HOW FiSH GET FOOD

Fish find food in many different ways. Some eat other fish. Others suck in tiny plants and animals that drift in the sea. Some eat seaweed and other plants. Still others dig in the seabed and eat the small creatures that live there.

A fish's mouth and teeth give clues to what it eats and how it gets its food.

The Common Lionfish swims slowly with its pectoral fins held out. The fins round up shrimps, and its mouth scoops them up. ▶

▲ A Half-and-Half Wrasse grubs in the sea floor for worms and other small creatures.

The Grey Nurse Shark's mouth opens widely. It feeds by ripping pieces out of animals. It may swallow them whole. As old teeth break, new ones take their place.

A MOUTH TO SUIT

Fish with bony skeletons have teeth that are fixed to their jaws. Sharks' teeth are not fixed. Their teeth often fall out or break and new teeth take their place. A shark's teeth are like sharp daggers.

A Long-Snout Boarfish finds food by poking its long snout ▲ into reef cracks and sand.

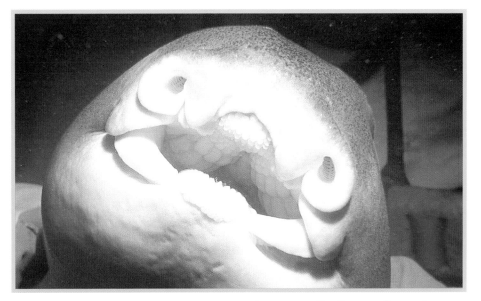

▲ The Port Jackson Shark has flat back teeth. It uses them to crush crabs, sea urchins, and other prey.

WHiSKERS AND SiDELiNES

Catfish and some other sorts of fish have fleshy whiskers called barbels around their mouths. These act as feelers and help the catfish find prey to eat.

All fish have lines of tiny cells along the sides of their bodies. These can feel changes in water pressure. They also help the fish hear low sounds.

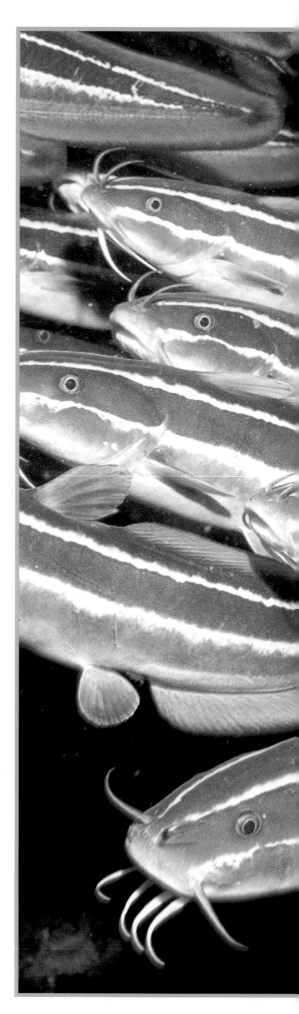

▲ An Estuary Catfish using its barbels to feel for food on the seabed.

▲ A school of Striped Catfish.

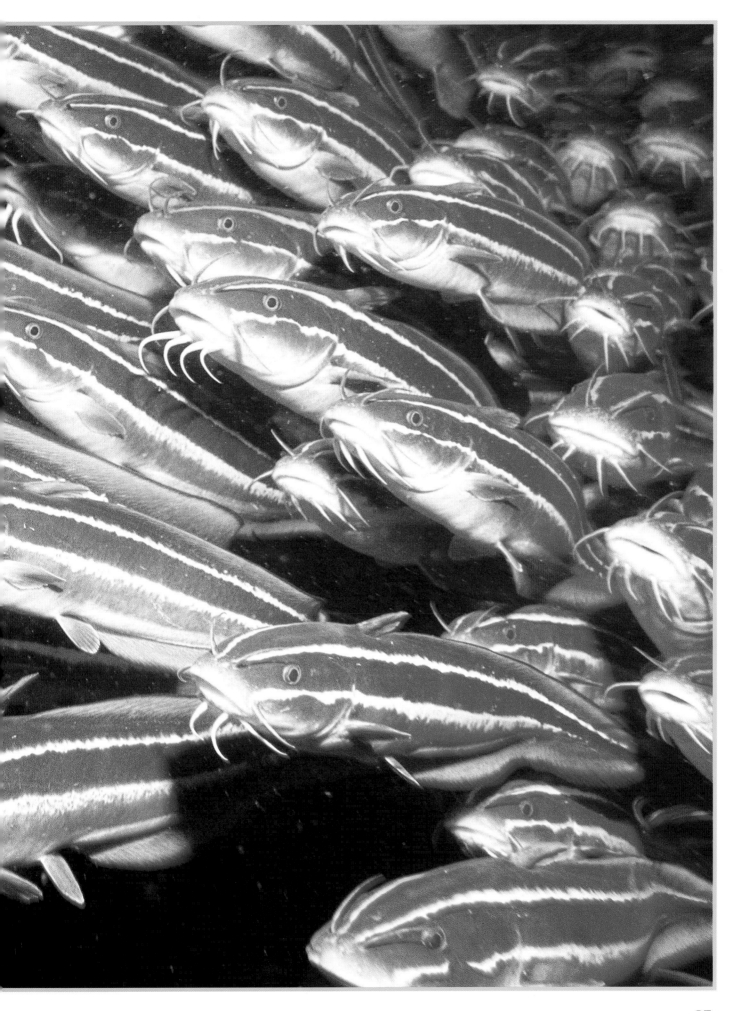

HOW FiSH KEEP CLEAN

A Beaked Coralfish and a ▲
Magpie Morwong being helped
by two Cleaner Wrasse.

◀ Cleaner Wrasse work on a
Barramundi Cod.

A fish has no hands. It cannot pull small pests from its body or fix its own wounds. When a large fish needs to have its skin looked after, it goes to a cleaning station. This is a place where small fish called cleaners live.

The large fish may have to wait its turn. Then the cleaner fish will pick all the pests from its body. It will also clean up any wounds. Sometimes, the cleaner goes inside the fish's gill slits and mouth. It even cleans the teeth.

FiSH ON CORAL REEFS

▲ Coral needs sunlight to grow.

Coral animals have tiny, soft bodies. They build little stony homes. Clumps of these homes form the coral that makes reefs.

Coral grows where the water is warm and clean. It needs sunlight, so it usually grows in quite shallow water.

The fish that live around coral reefs find all sorts of food on the coral and in the sand. When there is danger, the fish hide among the coral.

▲ Surgeonfish live around coral and eat tiny animals that float on the sea currents.

Many kinds of fish hide among coral. ▶

FISH ON SANDY SEA FLOORS

Fish that live on the sandy sea floor are often camouflaged in dull colors. They lie on the sand, waiting for prey to swim by.

Fish that dig in the sand to find food may have barbels, or feelers, on their heads. They cannot see their prey, but they can feel it and snap it up.

◀ A Southern Goatfish stirring up sand: It snaps up prey that it touches with its chin barbels.

▲ A Fiddler Ray hiding in the sand.

FiSH ON ROCKY REEFS

▲ The Black-Banded Seaperch shelters in rocky caves.

▲ A Red-Lip Morwong sleeping in a hollow in a rocky reef.

Around the south of Australia, the water is too cold for coral to grow. These coasts have rocky platforms and reefs. The waves on rocky coasts are often rough.

Some fish can live where the water rushes over rock platforms. Other fish live further out to sea where there are plenty of rock caves and cracks for shelter.

The center fish is a Maori Wrasse. ▶
The fish around it are Butterfly Perch.

44 ▲ A Big-Belly Seahorse shelters in a bed of seagrass. It eats tiny shrimps it finds there.

FISH IN SEAGRASS MEADOWS

Seagrass is found in clean, shallow water. It grows on sand or mud. Its tough leaves are often crusted with other tiny plants.

Many young fish live in seagrass beds. When they are big enough, they swim into the ocean. Other sea creatures that feed on seagrass include turtles and dugongs.

▲ Six-Spine Leatherjackets attack the seahorse.

FISH IN OPEN OCEANS

▲ Hardyheads swim in schools. A school of tiny fish can look like one big fish from a distance.

In the open ocean, there is no place to hide. Fish that live there must swim fast to escape enemies. Many fish swim in large schools. A small fish on its own is easy for a hunter to catch.

Fish that live in the open ocean are darker colored on their backs and lighter on their bellies. This protective color pattern makes them harder to see from above and from below.

◄ Big-Eye Trevally are fast swimmers.

FiSH THAT DO NOT LOOK LiKE FiSH

Sharks are fish. There are about 170 different sorts of sharks found in Australian seas.

Eels are fish. They have long, thin bodies, like snakes. Many eels have slimy skin without fish-like scales.

Seadragons and seahorses are also fish. Instead of scales, their bodies have bony plates, like armor.

▲ A Port Jackson Shark

A Weedy Seadragon ▶

▲ A Green Moray Eel out hunting.

INDEX OF ANIMALS PICTURED

FURTHER READING & INTERNET RESOURCES

For more information on Australia's animals, check out the following books and Web sites.

Cerullp, Mary M., Jeffrey L. Rotman (photographer), and Michael Wertz (illustrator). The Truth About Great White Sharks. (April 2000) Chronicle Books; ISBN: 0811824675

The great white shark—quite possibly Australia's most famous marine fish—is also a creature that is largely misunderstood. Learn how to separate the truth from the myths about great whites.

Spillman, David and Mark Wilson (illustrator). Yellow-Eye. (September 2001) Crocodile Books (Inteu); ISBN: 1566564107

When the numbers of the Yellow-Eye Fish begin to decline, white men and aborigines must work together to come up with a solution.

Arnold, Caroline. *Australian Animals*. (August 2000) HarperCollins Juvenile Books; ISBN: 0688167667

Seventeen unusual animals from Australia are introduced in this full-color book, including koalas, possums, gliders, quolls, Tasmanian devils, platypuses, echidnas, kangaroos, wombats, dingoes, snakes, and penguins.

Morpurgo, Michael, Christian Birmingham (illustrator). *Wombat Goes Walkabout.* (April 2000) Candlewick Press; ISBN: 0763611689

As Wombat wanders through the Australian bush in search of his mother, he encounters a variety of creatures demanding to know who he is and what he can do.

http://home.mira.net/~areadman/aussie.htm

This Web site contains a comprehensive listing of the marine fish of Australia, with further links to in-depth information about various species.

http://www.fishnet.com.au/fishfile.html

This Web site provides information on all types of fishes in Australia, from marine to salt water. Specific information is provided on the habitat, characteristics, and qualities of each type of fish.

http://www.wildlife-australia.com/

This Web site is actually for the Chambers Wildlife Rainforest Lodge in Queensland, Australia, but it provides hundreds of links to all sorts of Australian rainforest creatures. From frogs to birds, reptiles to butterflies, if it lives in the Australian rainforests, you'll find in-depth information on it here.

http://rainforest-australia.com/

This other Web site for Chambers Wildlife Rainforest Lodge contains even more extensive information and photos on Australia's rainforest animals. Find information on the different levels of the rainforest environment; see pictures of the various creatures that inhabit each layer; and learn about Australian animals, from dingoes to lizards and everything in between.

http://www.masseycreek.com/fauna_2.asp

Massey Creek, a tropical upland rainforest property, is in one of Australia's World Heritage areas. This Web site has general information accompanying photos of some of the animals that live there.

NATURE KIDS SERIES

Birdlife

Australia is home to some of the most interesting, colorful, and noisy birds on earth. Discover some of the many different types, including parrots, kingfishers, and owls.

Frogs and Reptiles

Australia has a wide variety of environments, and there is at least one frog or reptile that calls each environment home. Discover the frogs and reptiles living in Australia.

Kangaroos and Wallabies

The kangaroo is one of the most well-known Australian creatures. Learn interesting facts about kangaroos and wallabies, a close cousin.

Marine Fish

The ocean surrounding Australia is home to all sorts of marine fish. Discover their interesting shapes, sizes, and colors, and learn about the different types of habitat in the ocean.

Rainforest Animals

Australia's rainforests are home to a wide range of animals, including snakes, birds, frogs, and wallabies. Discover a few of the creatures that call the rainforests home.

Rare & Endangered Wildlife

Animals all over the world need our help to keep from becoming extinct. Learn about the special creatures in Australia that are in danger of disappearing forever.

Sealife

Australia is surrounded by sea. As a result, there is an amazing variety of life that lives in these waters. Dolphins, crabs, reef fish, and eels are just a few of the animals highlighted in this book.

Wildlife

Australia is known for its unique creatures, such as the kangaroo and the koala. Read about these and other special creatures that call Australia home.